Mail Order Marvel
Book 27 in Brides of Beckham
Kirsten Osbourne

Chapter One

CORAL ATE SLOWLY AS she peered at Jackson from under her lashes. She knew her sister, Esther, and her brother-in-law, Brody, both desperately wanted her to marry him, so she could move from their home. He didn't seem like a terrible person, and he was obviously intelligent. He'd do. As long as he'd agree to her terms, of course.

She listened to the other three talk as she ate the meal she'd overseen the preparations for. Her sister had only barely learned to cook, and she would have lots of difficulties once Coral was married and gone, but that didn't matter. She'd been married almost a week, and she still hadn't been able to consummate her marriage, because her sister lived there in her tiny little cabin.

Coral and Esther had grown up with money, but just seven weeks before, they'd discovered their father was an embezzler. Esther's fiancé, and the son of the man their father was embezzling from, had immediately called off their wedding, and Esther had agreed to be a mail order bride. She hadn't told her future husband, Brody, that she was bringing her sister along to live with them, though.

"Tell me about yourself, Coral," Jackson said, his voice strong and deep. It wasn't a question either. It was an order. He was demanding she tell him about herself.

"What do you want to know?" Coral asked, needing to learn about him, rather than disclose any information about herself at all. What if he wasn't the one she'd end up marrying? She didn't want him to know anything about her. She'd had enough gossip spread about her back in Massachusetts. She didn't need that nonsense here in Montana.

Jackson stared at her, noting that she still wasn't looking at him. Was she shy? "Anything you want to tell me. What do you like to do in your spare time?"

At that, Coral's eyes met his. "Back home I enjoyed studying anatomy text books and daydreaming that someday someone would allow me to become a doctor, even though I'm a woman. I doubt if I'll be able to continue that particular activity."

Jackson blinked a couple of times. He sensed something other than shyness in her voice. She didn't seem shy at all suddenly. No, she seemed angry. But at whom? "Why won't you continue? Did you not bring your books?"

Coral raised one eyebrow at him, the brown just a shade darker than her auburn hair. "I brought my books. I just have an inkling that whomever I end up married to will want his wife to do things he considers important, instead of reading about being a doctor, which will never happen in this world."

"Why won't it? You don't think you're capable?" Jackson asked, knowing he was going to annoy her with the question, but unable to stop it from escaping his lips. It was how he motivated his students.

"I *know* I'm capable. I just don't think anyone else will believe I'm capable, because I'm a female."

He shrugged. "There has to be a first for everything. Do you think the first man who said he could move west and ranch was believed? If you think you can, then you've fought ninety percent of the battle." He finished his meal and thanked her when dessert was put before him.

After eating her delicious gingerbread, he pushed away from the table and invited her to walk with him.

As they walked away from the house, he was aware they could be watched from the windows of the small cabin. He knew her sister and brother-in-law had invested a lot of hope on the two of them getting married, but he wasn't sure how they'd do together. Coral was obviously intelligent, a trait he admired, but she was also headstrong. He would have preferred a malleable wife.

"So I hear you need to marry," he said, refusing to beat around the bush with the woman. "I enjoyed your dessert. Do you cook as well as you bake?"

Coral gave a brief nod. "I'm an excellent cook. In fact, I think you'll find I excel at everything I do."

He laughed briefly. "No one is good at everything."

"So I've been told," she said, refusing to argue with the man.

"But *you're* good at everything?"

She nodded again. "Maybe it's only my perception, though." Of course, she knew it wasn't. She'd even heard her sister and Brody laughing at how good she was at everything, as if it was a fault, when she knew darn well it wasn't.

Jackson stared at her for a moment, looking her up and down. She wasn't classically pretty. Her hair was red, and she was covered in freckles. She was rounder than was fashionable, but her eyes were absolutely stunning. She'd do. He didn't need a beauty anyway. He just needed someone who would cook his meals and be a good companion. She'd surely have opinions on everything, and be willing to debate whenever he needed a good argument. While he'd prefer someone who would recognize his authority in everything, a woman who could hold her own may be just what he needed.

"Why are you in such a hurry to marry?" he asked. "There is such an overwhelming ratio of men to women here, you'd have no trouble finding a husband if you'd just let nature take its course."

She sighed at his words. "That's what I thought when we left Massachusetts, but Esther and Brody's marriage isn't going to work if I stay much longer. I'm in the way." She didn't mention the fact that the couple hadn't been able to consummate their marriage, but she knew he'd understand.

"I see. How old are you?" he asked. She seemed so smart, but really, she didn't look much older than some of his students.

"I'm seventeen. My eighteenth birthday is in November. I don't really think anyone should marry before they turn eighteen, but I don't feel like I have a choice. I would ask that you'd wait to consummate the marriage for that long if you do decide to marry me." She started to tell him that normally she wouldn't be so frank about such an intimate topic, but she stopped herself. Why lie?

"Is that a proposal?"

Coral refused to blush, which she knew had to be the only reason for his words. No, she wouldn't give him the pleasure of getting embarrassed. "If you want it to be, it is. Do you want to marry me?"

He blinked, surprised that Coral hadn't reacted to his teasing. Most women would rather be tortured than ask a man to marry them. "I can't wait to tell our children that their mother proposed to me within an hour and a half of meeting me."

"I guess that's a yes?"

He nodded, not certain if he enjoyed her frankness or was put off by it. "When do you want to do it?"

"Could we make it to Lost Legacy and back before you have to go to school on Monday morning?"

He pursed his lips, thinking about it. "I'm relatively certain we can make it work. We'll both be tired Monday, but it can't be helped."

Coral stepped toward him, knowing she was being forward, but just not caring. "You don't think you should kiss me to seal the engagement?"

He looked down at her, surprised by how pretty her upturned face looked to him by the light of the full moon overhead. "Do you think that's wise? If we're not going to consummate for two months, shouldn't we wait to start kissing?"

"Don't you want to know that we're compatible?"

He laughed. "We're compatible. I don't need to kiss you to know that."

Coral took a step back, surprised that she was disappointed. Obviously, he found the idea of kissing her to be a chore. What a way to start a marriage. "Let's go tell Esther and Brody then. If we're getting such an early start, surely you need to go home and sleep."

She turned on her heel and strode toward the house, not looking back at him. If Jackson didn't want to kiss her, then she had no reason to stand with him in the dark. The man already made her crazy.

Jackson hurried to catch up with her, realizing he'd hurt her feelings by not wanting to kiss her. He hadn't explained it well. "Coral, wait. It's not that I don't *want* to kiss you."

Coral shrugged and kept walking, until he caught her hand and pulled her to a stop. "What?"

"I don't want to start kissing you and then have to stop. I don't think it's a good idea for us to get our passions all riled up, and then have to wait for two months."

She nodded briefly, not meeting his eyes. "I understand."

"Your voice tells me you understand, but your body language is saying differently. I don't think you *do* understand."

"Does it really matter? You're getting your cook. I'm getting out of my sister's house, so she can be a newlywed. Nothing else really matters, does it?"

"Yes, it does. I don't want to hurt your feelings with this." He watched her face, but she kept her eyes downcast, so he couldn't read them. "I'll kiss you." He pulled her to him with the hand he still held, his free hand moving to tilt her chin up.

Coral turned her face away. "I'm not going to kiss an unwilling man. What kind of girl do you think I am?"

He wanted to laugh, knowing he'd already made a mess of things. "Just let me kiss you once, so I can put your fears to rest."

"What fears? I told you, I'm good at everything, which means I'm afraid of nothing. Let's go inside and tell my sister the good news."

He sighed. If she didn't want to kiss him, then she didn't want to kiss him. He didn't want to kiss her anyway, did he? Then why did he suddenly feel so disappointed?

He kept her hand in his, and she half-dragged him back to the house. For such a short woman, she was very strong. He wasn't sure if he liked that or not. He wanted her to feel like she needed him to keep her safe.

When they reached the house, Esther and Brody were standing close but they jumped apart as if embarrassed to be found that way. Coral quickly explained the situation.

The plans were made for him to return to get her at four the following morning, and he left quickly, not trying to kiss Coral again. The woman was being downright persnickety about that, and he wasn't going to fight her for the privilege.

Coral ignored all the arguments from her sister and went to the sink, rolling up her sleeves.

When Esther sent her to bed, she went willingly. She knew she wouldn't really sleep that night, but she had to at least try. Why, she was getting married. Tomorrow or Sunday at the latest.

She went to the room she shared with Esther and pulled her dress off, quickly changing into her nightgown. It was eight, and four would come very early. She packed up all of her things into the two carpet bags she'd brought with her from Massachusetts before climbing into the bed and rolling onto her side.

Her tears fell as soon as she was covered up to her chin. How could she possibly marry a man who didn't even want to kiss her? Their lives together would never be worth anything. Oh how she wished she had time to just be a young woman and court whomever came along.

It wasn't that she didn't like Jackson, of course. She did. She just didn't want to feel forced into a marriage.

She took a deep breath and closed her eyes. Tomorrow would be a new day. Tomorrow she would be strong. Tomorrow would be a blessing. It always was.

Chapter Two

WAKING EARLIER THAN necessary after a fitful night's sleep, Coral hurriedly carried her carpet bags into the main room of the cabin to wait for Jackson. She wanted to put her face in her hands and sob, but what if someone heard her? No, she wouldn't show weakness. She couldn't. She was a bride, whether she wanted to be or not.

When she heard Jackson's buggy pull up into the yard, she hurried outside, wishing she had someone to ride along with them as a chaperone. She wasn't afraid of him, but it wasn't natural to be alone with a man she wasn't married to. Well, it didn't feel natural to *her* anyway. She'd always been very strict with her moral code for herself, worried she'd take after her birth mother in every way.

Jackson didn't get down from the buggy, but he did offer her a hand and help her up. She threw her bag into the back, smoothed her skirts, and covered herself with the lap robe he was already under. "How did you sleep?" he asked, his voice sounding deeper than it had the night before.

Coral felt a shiver travel up her spine. His voice did things to her that she could never admit to. "Fine," she lied. She wasn't about to tell her fiancé that she'd spent the entire night tossing and turning, trying to figure out how she could leave her sister's house but still not marry yet. She'd come to no conclusions.

Jackson drove out onto the road, looking at Coral out of the corner of his eye. Something was wrong, but he had no idea what it was. "That's good." What did one say to the woman he was about to marry, when one knew almost nothing about her?

Coral sighed, wishing things weren't quite so awkward between them. "What are you getting out of this?" she asked bluntly, knowing she'd either offend him, and he'd turn the buggy around and take her right back to her sister, or it would break the ice between them. She wasn't certain which she preferred at that moment.

He frowned, wondering if she would always say exactly what was on her mind. "I'm a terrible cook," he admitted. "I hate doing household chores. I want to be able to teach all day and come home to a clean house and supper on the table."

"Well, that's honest." She stared off into the darkness, knowing the sun wouldn't be up for a couple of hours yet. "I can do those things."

"And eventually, I'll have a wife to warm my bed and children."

She swallowed hard at his words. "But not until after I turn eighteen, right? And we get used to each other?" She hated the idea of going straight to his bed, even though she was strongly attracted to him. The woman who had given birth to her had been her father's mistress. She considered her mother to be the woman who had raised her and her father's wife. She had no desire to be like her birth mother—a woman whose life was ruled by passion.

At least, that's what she assumed her birth mother was like. She'd never met the woman.

Jackson shook his head. "Of course not. I gave you my word." He was offended that she would even question him. A man's word should never be questioned by his wife. Then he sighed. The woman barely knew him. Of course, she wouldn't simply take him at his word. How could she? "I'll install a lock on your door if necessary."

Coral looked over at him in the darkness. "You have two bedrooms then?"

He shook his head. "I'm afraid not. I have just the one. If you're not comfortable sharing the bed with me platonically, then I will make a bed on the floor in the main room."

She frowned. "I don't like the idea of you sleeping on the floor, but I'm not sure how I feel about sharing a bed either. Give me a little while, and I'll let you know."

"Fair enough." He glanced over at her, noticing that she was sitting ramrod straight on the seat beside him. She'd never make it all the way to Lost Legacy if she held herself so rigidly. He was worried for her. "I'm not going to bite you."

She glanced at him, surprised by his words. "Why do you say that?"

He shrugged. "You just seem very tense. I've never seen someone sit up so straight when they didn't have to."

"Really? I don't see a reason to do anything halfway. If you're going to do it, you may as well do it right."

Was she really that rigid in thinking as well as posture? No wonder her sister and brother-in-law hadn't been able to wait to get rid of her. "Why fatigue yourself when you could rest? If you want, you can use my shoulder to rest against. I'll drive while you sleep."

As tired as she was, the offer was tempting. "No thank you. I'm fine." She couldn't show him, or anyone else, weakness. Maybe eventually, but not as soon as they met. "Tell me about your family. How did you end up teaching in Montana?"

"My mother and step-father moved to Montana when I was twelve. I was already mostly through with my schooling, because I worked as many hours as I could to finish early. When we moved out here, I helped with the farm chores as much as I could, while continuing to study in the evenings." He shrugged. "It didn't take me long to determine that I had no desire to be a farmer. I didn't like the idea of relying on the fickle weather for my well-being, so I applied to teach. I took a couple of jobs locally, and I enjoyed them, but I realized that I wanted to teach where there was a greater need for teachers. In a place where students would either have me or no education at all. So when I saw the community here was looking for a teacher, I applied.

"Are you glad you did? How long have you been at your current post?" Her mind started racing. Did that mean he'd be looking for other positions? Would she lose her sister after all?

He nodded. "I love it here. I have no intention of going anywhere."

She wondered if he had read her fears. She hoped not, because having a husband who knew when she was afraid would be downright frightening. She didn't want anyone to have that sort of power over her. "I'm glad. I believe I'd like to stay in close proximity to my sister."

"I take it the two of you are close?"

Coral shrugged, not quite certain how to answer that. "We've always looked out for one another." The truth was that they'd never been particularly close. They were too different. Esther had always been a fashion plate, interested in only the latest dress and whom she would marry. Coral's mind wasn't given to frivolous things like that.

Jackson read between the lines, understanding that the sisters hadn't been close. How odd that Coral was determined to stay near her sister then. "Tell me about your parents."

Coral debated simply telling him the story she'd believed when she was young but decided he deserved the full truth before they married. "Esther and I are half-sisters. I'm the daughter of our father's mistress. We're less than a year apart. When my father told my mother that I was on the way, she agreed to pretend to be pregnant, and then she raised me as if I was her own."

Jackson raised an eyebrow at that. "She did? There was no resentment or favoritism?"

"I'm sure there was some, but not so anyone on the outside would notice. After my birth, Mother became a bit of a recluse. She didn't go out and do all the fun things she'd done leading up to my arrival. She wasn't willing to admit she'd been thwarted by her own husband."

"So she was cruel to you?"

"Never! She was kind, the same as she was to Esther. She just—well, Esther got more of her *attention*. She had Mother's approval. It was always clear that no one was very interested in me. I was the not-as-pretty, not-as-slim, not-as-socially-acceptable younger sister, who was a slight embarrassment to the family." She shrugged. "I helped them out by spending most of my time with my nose buried in a book, and then they didn't have to acknowledge me. I made friends with the servants and learned to cook. I really learned anything anyone was willing to teach me."

"I admire that." Jackson was surprised to realize he did. The girl beside him was slightly frightening with as much as she knew about everything around her, but she was also a marvel, in her own way. She was obviously highly intelligent, and no matter that she'd been born into less-than-ideal circumstances, she was a bold, confident woman.

"Do you really? Or does it make you uncomfortable?"

"Why would it make me uncomfortable?"

She shrugged. "I have no earthly idea. It makes everyone *else* uncomfortable though. People look at me as if I'm some sort of oddity, and they don't quite know what to say or do around me. Like I'm some sort of super-human, and everything I do is because it's easy, and not hard work."

"And it's not easy?"

She frowned. "I wouldn't go so far to say that. I do learn things, and become good at things, much faster and easier than other people do. But that doesn't make me any less human. When I see something is going to be difficult for me, I give it everything I have. I work twice as hard, so that I can be as good. People don't see that, though. They just see someone who excels at everything."

He nodded. "I can understand that." He was slightly surprised by her words, because it was just how he felt about almost everything. "I do much of the same thing."

"You do?" She turned to him, barely able to make out his features in the pre-dawn darkness.

"Of course I do." She didn't think he'd lie about something so small, did she? They would have to build trust between them if they were to ever get along.

She smiled. "I'm glad to hear we have something in common then. Maybe this one small thing will grow to something more."

He smiled at that, transferring the reins into his left hand, and moving his right hand to cover hers in her lap. "I certainly hope so. I would hate for the two of us to be forced to live together for the next fifty years with no feelings between us."

"That would truly be a tragic life to live, wouldn't it?" She shook her head. She couldn't imagine living the rest of her life with no love. She'd already lived the first part of it with no one finding her special or good enough. She needed to have someone who thought she was wonderful. Someone who would call her dear, and hold her hand when the situation called for it. "I think I'm glad you're the one who I'm going to marry, Jackson."

He jerked, staring down at her. "You are?" He'd never expected to hear any sort of kindness from her lips.

She nodded. "There's something about you that I think I can spend the rest of my life being happy with. I hope so anyway."

He squeezed the hand he still held. "I'll do my best to make you happy, Coral. I make no promises, because I'm inept at everything where women are concerned, but I do think you're special. We'll make a good team."

"I do believe we will. I have a feeling you won't mind if I spend time pouring over the medical treatises I have, and that will be a good start."

He laughed. "As long as you promise to use anything you learn on me should I become ill."

"Oh, there's no doubt. I shall endeavor to keep you very healthy." She smiled as she stared straight ahead into the darkness. The man beside her wasn't nearly as difficult as she'd thought he would be. Why, he was downright pleasant now that they'd spent a bit more time together. Maybe the future wasn't as bleak as she'd imagined it would be.

Chapter Three

IT WAS ALMOST EIGHT that night when they arrived in Lost Legacy, and Jackson drove straight to the preacher's house. "I don't want us to spend a night alone together until we've been officially married."

Coral agreed, not wanting anything to possibly mar her reputation in her new home. Her legs were cramped as she allowed him to help her down from the buggy, and it was all she could do not to cry out. They'd only made necessary stops along the way, preferring to eat as they drove. "I think that's for the best."

Jackson knew how hard it was for his legs to support him after their long journey, so he watched her face carefully for any sign of pain, but she showed nothing. "Have you met Pastor and Mrs. Sands yet?"

"Yes, I met them when Esther and I arrived in town. He married Brody and Esther."

"Oh, of course. I didn't think of that." Jackson took hold of her elbow, still worried she might fall after the long drive in cramped quarters. "I hope he's willing to perform our ceremony this late."

"Me too." Coral didn't know what she'd do if he said he wouldn't marry them so late at night. She couldn't ask Jackson to pay for an extra room for her, and she wouldn't feel right spending a night in the same room with him before they married.

When Mrs. Sands opened the door, she stared at them blankly for a moment, and then she smiled. "Coral, isn't it?"

"Yes, ma'am. I'm here to get married myself this time."

Mrs. Sands smiled, opening the door wide. "The pastor is still working on his sermon for tomorrow, but he won't mind the interruption. Please have a seat." She hurried from the room, presumably to get her husband.

Coral walked around the small parlor, trying to get her legs to work correctly again.

Jackson watched her and understood what she was doing immediately. "I'm sorry we have to push so hard to get home by Sunday night."

She stopped her pacing and shook her head. "No, there's nothing to be sorry for. We're doing what we need to do. If we had to, we could start driving back tonight."

He walked to her taking her hand in his. "Life won't always be hard," he promised.

She shrugged. "From what I can see, it is." And it had been for her. Maybe it would be easier now that they were about to be married, but she didn't see how it could be. They'd just be two people working side by side, not a couple who found comfort in one another's presence. Not like Esther and Brody. She felt her eyes sting, as if tears wanted to fall, but she fought them back. No, she wasn't going to cry in front of him. Or anyone else for that matter.

Jackson watched her uncertainly. "It won't be any more." He hoped it was true. He could see that together they could do wonderful things. If only she would stop being so strong for everyone.

The pastor and Mrs. Sands came back into the room then. "So, you two want to be married, do you?"

Jackson nodded. "I'm not sure if you remember me, sir?"

"Oh, but I do! You visited my church a couple of times before you left for your little country school. Have you set up your own congregation there as you were hoping to do?"

"Not yet, but I plan to do it soon. Right now I'm still getting used to being in the classroom." He waved his hand toward Coral. "I understand you've already met my bride?"

Pastor Sands nodded. "She was here recently with her older sister. It's good to see you again. I'm sorry, but I've forgotten your name."

"I'm not exactly memorable," Coral said, trying to get her red curls back into the pins that kept them atop her head. "I'm Coral."

"Are you two ready to start?"

Coral looked down at herself, wishing she'd changed as soon as they got there. She didn't feel like she could now, because she didn't want to keep everyone waiting. "Yessir. I'm ready."

Jackson nodded, moving over to stand beside his bride. "Let's get it done."

Coral wrinkled her nose at his less than romantic words, but really, what did she expect? They were marrying for reasons other than love, and she had no right to expect him to act as if it was any other way.

She paid careful attention to the vows, agreeing to love, honor, and cherish him. She was relieved she hadn't been asked to obey, because she'd have had to say no to that. She wasn't obeying anyone as if she didn't have a brain in her head to think for herself.

When Pastor Sands told Jackson to kiss her, she turned to Jackson, wondering what he'd do. He put his hands on her shoulders and pulled her to him, his lips coming down on hers gently.

Coral was surprised at the rush of feeling that went through her at the touch of Jackson's lips on hers. She'd always assumed the one thing in life she'd be bad at was passion, but apparently her birth mother had left her something. She put her hands on his shoulders and kissed him back, a tingling starting at her spine and running down her body.

Jackson lifted his head, looking down into his bride's face, stunned at her reaction to him. He'd expected her to be cold and unfeeling, but that was just the opposite of what she'd given him. Her eyes were half-closed, and her lips slightly parted. It was all he could do not to lean down and kiss her again.

He stepped back, clearing his throat, embarrassed all at once. He'd promised to wait two months before he consummated the marriage. It was going to be the longest two months of his life.

Coral opened her eyes fully to see Jackson staring at her as if she were a stranger. "I guess we'd better be on our way," she mumbled, trying to cover just what his kiss had done to her.

Jackson shook himself out of his reverie. "Yes, of course. We have to find a place to stay for the night yet." He turned and shook hands with the pastor, paying him for performing the ceremony.

The pastor looked at his wife and back at Jackson. "You know we don't have a hotel in Lost Legacy, don't you?"

Jackson nodded. "I was hoping for a boarding house or something."

"Not that'll take you at this time of night." The pastor looked at Mrs. Sands. "How 'bout it?"

Mrs. Sands nodded immediately. "We have a spare room. Of course you'll stay!"

"Oh, but we couldn't!" Coral protested. She'd seen the tiny little bed in that room when she'd been there with Esther. No, that wouldn't work at all.

Jackson cleared his throat. "It's that or sleep outside tonight."

Coral's shoulders sagged. He was right. They'd have to stay there. They could make it work. She nodded. "We'd be happy to accept your hospitality, Mrs. Sands."

Jackson put his arm around her shoulders casually. "We'll have to be up before the sun so we can get on the road, though."

"Oh, I wish you had time to stay for church, but I understand. Have you eaten tonight? We have some supper left. I made a pot roast and mashed potatoes."

Coral looked at Jackson, waiting for his response. Her stomach was growling, but she didn't want to be the only one eating. She felt like they were asking too much just by staying there.

Jackson nodded. "We'd be much obliged, ma'am. We had sandwiches six hours ago while we drove."

"Oh, you should have said something sooner." Mrs. Sands hurried off to the kitchen to reheat the food.

Coral followed after her. "May I help?"

"Just set the table for the two of you, dear."

Coral went to work setting the table while the older woman reheated the food. The smells that were coming from the stove made her even hungrier, and she wanted to insist it was too much work to heat things up. They'd just eat it cold. If she'd truly been worried about the work involved, she'd have done just that, but she knew she only wanted to eat sooner.

Ten minutes later, Coral and Jackson were sitting across from one another at the table in the Sands' kitchen. The pastor and Mrs. Sands joined them, and the pastor was grinning from ear to ear. "Mrs. Sands doesn't let me have a second dessert unless we have company eating here late. Tonight I get two pieces of her delicious pie."

Mrs. Sands frowned at her husband. "Now you know you can always have another piece of pie if you want one."

"But you won't make me coffee to go with it if no one is here to help me drink it."

Coral grinned at Jackson, taking in the banter of the older couple. She wondered if they too would be like that in forty or so years.

They ate quickly and retired to the tiny room Mrs. Sands gave them. Coral eyed the bed skeptically, but refused to worry about it.

Jackson frowned when he saw their bed for the night but waited until the door was closed before expressing his worry. "I'm not sure about that bed."

Coral closed her eyes for a moment and then said, "I'll sleep under the sheet, and you sleep over it. It will be fine. It's not like we're incapable of suppressing our baser urges."

Jackson shrugged. "Are you sure you'll be comfortable with that?"

She nodded. "Of course I will." She looked at him. "Could you please turn your back while I put my nightgown on?"

He nodded, presenting his back immediately. He listened to the rustle of her clothing as she changed, wishing he could turn around and just watch. They were married after all. "Let me know when you're finished."

Coral hurried and slid between the sheets before saying anything. "I'm ready."

Jackson was disappointed to find her in the bed with the sheets pulled up to her neck. "Now it's your turn to turn your back." Truthfully, he didn't care if she saw him undressing or not, but he didn't want to make her uncomfortable.

He slid into bed beside her, careful to keep as much distance between them as he could. He reached over and turned down the lamp before closing his eyes. "Goodnight, Coral."

Coral sighed, wishing she had something witty to say to the man lying beside her—her new husband. "Goodnight, Jackson." Her eyes were already drifting closed. They'd had such a long day after a sleepless night. How on earth could she be expected to carry on any kind of conversation with him?

Jackson stared at the ceiling, not sure if he wanted her to say something else or go straight to sleep. On one hand, if she said something else, she'd probably insist that he kiss her again. She was a bossy little thing. On the other, if she asked him to kiss her again, well—then he could kiss her again. He had just opened his mouth to suggest to her that he should kiss her goodnight, now that they were married, when he heard her even breathing.

He looked over at her, and sure enough, she was sound asleep beside him. It had been a long day. He closed his eyes as well, determined to leave for home as early as they could the following morning. It was going to be another long, long day. Alone. With his new wife.

Chapter Four

BY THE TIME JACKSON pulled into the yard of his small home the following evening, both he and Coral were exhausted. "I'll fix something to eat," she said, getting down from the wagon while he went to unhitch the horses and put them up.

"Just something easy."

Coral nodded and went into the house, her new home, for the first time. She was surprised at how tiny the place was. She wanted to cry when she saw how little space she'd have to live in, but she shook her head, refusing to get upset. Instead, she pulled her apron from her bag and put it on, pinned her hair back up, and rolled up her sleeves.

The house wasn't filthy, but neither was it clean. She'd have a few days of backbreaking work to get it to the point where she felt it should be. She did the few dishes in the sink before rummaging around for food. She found some fresh eggs and some bacon, so she immediately whipped up scrambled eggs with small chunks of bacon in it. It wasn't fancy, but she was too tired to do anything more than that.

When Jackson came into the house, he hung his hat on a hook by the door, and took off his jacket. It was only September, but it was already getting a bit nippy in the evenings. "That smells good."

She smiled at him. "It's just eggs with some bacon chunks."

"I'm hungry, so that sounds delicious." He wished he could find the right way to convey how he felt about her cooking for him. He'd tried so hard to learn during his years as a teacher, but he'd gotten nowhere. Perhaps being able to cook was in a person's genes, and he'd been born without that particular gene.

He washed his hands and face using water from the pump and then sat down at the table, waiting.

Coral put his plate on the table in front of him and sat down with her own plate. They each had a cup of water to drink. "Do you have a cow?" she asked.

He nodded. "I took it to one of my students to take care of while we were gone."

She hadn't considered he'd had arrangements to make before they could leave. "Well, it'll be nice to have fresh milk."

"I have several chickens as well, as I'm sure you've gathered."

She nodded. "I figured as much. I'll be thankful for the eggs for my cooking." She looked down at her plate for a moment, hesitant to bring up something she needed to talk to him about. "I think we can keep sleeping like we did last night. With you on top of the sheet and me under it. It worked well." Sort of. It had been a bit awkward, of course, but not so awkward they couldn't stand it.

"Are you sure?" He looked over at her, trying to read her face, but she was looking down at her plate, hiding her eyes from him. "I can make a bed on the floor if I need to."

She shook her head. "I'm sure. I'm not a shrinking violet." She finished her food and walked to the sink, immediately washing the dishes she'd dirtied. "I'm going to need to get more food as well. I'm happy to have eggs and milk, but unless you have flour and sugar and other basic ingredients hidden somewhere I can't find, I'm going to need to go to town."

He frowned. "I didn't think of that. I can take you into Mangled Stump after school tomorrow if you'd like." He would have to put off grading some papers, but he could still make it work.

"I thought that was several hours away by wagon."

He nodded. "It is, but if we need supplies, we need supplies."

"Would you mind if I took the buggy on my own? If you hitched it up before you went to work in the morning, I would get home in the afternoon, about when you would be able to unhitch it again."

He thought it over for a moment before nodding. "I'll draw you a map of how to get there in the morning. It's not difficult if you just keep following the main road."

"That would help a great deal if you don't mind."

"I don't mind at all. I like to eat. More than I should probably."

She smiled at that. "Well, I'll be sure to keep you fed if you can keep me in supplies."

"I'll leave you with some money as well. I don't make a whole lot, but we can sure afford whatever food you want to buy."

"That's all we need."

He nodded. "All right." He stood up. "I'll stay outside for twenty minutes or so to give you time to get ready for bed."

"Thank you." She hurriedly finished the dishes and put them away before going into the bedroom and changing. She was thankful he was so thoughtful.

She was asleep as soon as her head hit the pillow, exhausted from her long days of travel. Being married was hard work.

DRIVING THE BUGGY TO town was an interesting experience for Coral. Jackson had her drive him to school, so she could get a feel for the horses, and then she just kept driving. She wished she had time to scrub the house before going for supplies, but it made sense to get food right away. She couldn't invite herself and her new husband to her sister's house for every meal while she got her new home cleaned.

While she drove, she let her mind flow, thinking about the past couple of days. When she'd first met Jackson, she'd found him to be too rigid. He was very schoolteacherish in her mind. Now that she'd spent time with him, though, she realized that it wasn't so much that he was rigid, but more that he was uncomfortable with new situations. Having someone interested in marrying him was very new. Being married was new.

As they got to know each other more, she realized that she could come to care for him. All the things about her that others found odd, he liked. He was something like she was in that regard. He'd finished school young, and was very intelligent. They both had a love for learning, which she couldn't discount.

No, she was certain that if she had to marry immediately, she'd found a good man to be her husband.

When she got to town, she went into the mercantile, buying the supplies necessary for a couple of weeks' worth of cooking. She immediately turned around and headed home afterward, knowing she would have to make pancakes or something equally simple for dinner again. She didn't want to have to keep making such quick meals, and she wouldn't have to any longer now that she had the ingredients she would need for something more complex.

When she pulled into the yard, Jackson came out of the house. "I was starting to wonder if I should worry about you!" he called.

She scrambled down from the buggy after setting the break. "No need to worry. It's a long drive."

"I know. I needed to know my wife was all right though." He walked close to her, taking her hand in his. "I had to worry at least a little."

She blushed at his attention. "I'm fine."

"I'm glad." He looked into her eyes for a moment, and then did what he'd been wanting to do since the wedding ceremony. He leaned down and brushed his lips across hers, needing to know if what he'd felt that night was real, or just a faulty memory.

When her hands wound around his back and her lips parted for his, he knew it wasn't a faulty memory. She felt a great deal of passion for him, just as he felt for her. He sighed, resting his forehead against hers. "I'm not sure how I'm going to wait two months."

His words were soft, but she heard them, blushing profusely. "I—I got everything we needed at the store in town."

He grinned slightly at her change of subject. Obviously she wasn't ready for talk of passion yet, but soon. He needed her to understand he hadn't married her only for her cooking skills. "I'll help you carry everything in."

He released her, reaching behind the seat of the buggy to get some of her purchases, while she went around and got more from the other side. Together they carried them in, and while he unhitched the horses, and then graded papers, she scrubbed out the cabinets and put the supplies away.

"I'm going to have to make something simple tonight, because I didn't have time to start a big meal. Do you want pancakes or eggs?"

"Let's have pancakes tonight, if you don't mind." She'd made eggs for him twice in the past twenty-four hours. He wasn't complaining, because he hadn't had to cook, but he would be happy to have something else.

"I don't mind a bit. Do you want to drink milk with them or would you rather have coffee?" She saw a bucket of milk sitting on the work table that he had obviously gotten for her.

"Milk is fine. I prefer not to have coffee in the evenings, because it keeps me awake at night."

She made a mental note of his preference and went to work on the pancakes. "What are you working on?" she asked.

"I'm grading papers. I didn't do any over the weekend, so I have a surplus of papers that need to be addressed today."

"Maybe I could help?" She felt funny asking, because she had no idea how he'd feel about it, but she was more than willing. It would be nice to use her brain for something more than how to get a stain out of clothing.

"Have you ever graded papers before?"

She shook her head. "No, but I'm sure I could do it."

He studied her for a moment before nodding. "I'd like it if you'd help me."

"After supper dishes then." She turned away from him, trying to hide her smile. She loved the idea that he'd let her help with something he considered important, and she'd be doing more than just feeding him and keeping his house clean.

An hour later, she had all the dishes put away and joined him at the table. "How can I help?"

He gave her a stack of papers. "I gave a math test to my oldest students today. I graded the first, so you just need to use that as a guide and grade the others according to it."

She nodded, her eyes immediately skimming over the test. "Wait. There's an error in the first, and you didn't mark it."

"I used the teacher's manual. There can't be." He took the test from her and looked at it, a smile curving his lips. "There *is* an error! Thank you for catching that." He marked the problem off and changed the grade at the top. "Do you even need an answer key?"

She shook her head. "No. I do arithmetic at an alarming speed in my head." She looked down as she said it, knowing girls weren't supposed to be good at math.

"That's wonderful! I sometimes get confused with some of the more advanced math. I'm better with poetry and literature. I may let you come in and teach some of that."

"Really?" she asked. "I'd love to!"

He grinned. "I'd love the help. There are only so many things a person can excel at, and math has never been one of those things for me."

"I really do excel at everything. I'm not sure if it's a gift or a curse."

Jackson studied her, believing her more than he had the first time she'd said that to him. "Well, I'm glad you're mine then, because I definitely have flaws."

Coral laughed. "Oh, I didn't say I don't have flaws. I have many flaws. I'm just good at everything, which some consider a flaw right there."

"Not me. I think you're pretty wonderful."

Her eyes met his, and she blushed, looking down at the paper in front of her. "I'll get started then."

He grinned. "You do that."

Chapter Five

CORAL WOKE EARLY AND got to work fixing breakfast the next morning. She needed to bake bread and get the laundry taken care of, so it was going to be a busy morning.

Jackson woke shortly after the sun was up and looked at the empty spot beside him on the bed. His new wife was truly an amazing woman. She was up before him every day. She had graded the math papers faster than he'd ever done without an answer key. She didn't intimidate him, exactly, because how could a seventeen-year-old girl do so? She did make him wonder how she'd become so good at everything she did, though.

When he walked into the main room of the house, he found her up to her elbows in bread dough. "Good morning," he said, still rubbing the sleep from his eyes.

"Good morning." Her eyes stayed on the bread dough she was kneading, but her heart started racing at his presence. "Breakfast is in the oven keeping warm. Give me a minute to wash up, and I'll serve it for you."

"We're not in a hurry. I need to go out and milk Lizzie anyway."

"Lizzie? Is that the cow's name? I've already taken care of that."

"Then I'll collect the eggs."

She nodded to a basket of eggs on the work table. "Already done."

"Then I'll step outside for a bit of sunshine before breakfast." *How long has the woman been up? Doesn't she need sleep?* He was feeling like a sloth in comparison, a feeling he'd never had before.

"Okay, but don't take long. Breakfast will be on the table in ten minutes."

Jackson stepped outside and went to the outhouse to take care of personal business. After walking back to the house, he leaned against the side, breathing deeply. He loved mornings. The air seemed fresher, and he always felt so hopeful with the whole day spread out before him. He didn't know if he'd gotten the feeling from his time on the farm with his step-father, but he was sure the man hadn't hurt any. He'd been a jovial man to work with, and Jackson thanked God every day that he was the one his mother had chosen to marry after his father's untimely demise.

Shaking his head, he opened the door to the house and walked straight to the pump to wash his hands. "What are your plans for the day?" he asked.

Coral was surprised by the question. Did men usually ask their wives how they planned to stay busy? "I'm going to catch up on the laundry, bake bread, give the house a good fall cleaning, including blacking the stove and washing down all the walls. I'll make supper. If I have time left, I'll bake a cake and scrub the floors. I wish I had time to do the windows today, but those will have to wait until tomorrow."

He shook his head. "You know you don't have to do everything today, don't you? You have the rest of your life to clean and cook."

She nodded. "I do know. I want to get a good start on the chores, though. I can do things I'll enjoy once everything here is caught up. I'd like to go visit my sister, but I won't do it until the house is in ship-shape condition."

He took his seat at the table and waited as she brought him his plate. Eggs, bacon and biscuits. The biscuits looked so fluffy, he couldn't wait to sink his teeth into one of them. "You can visit her any time you want. I'm not trying to keep you from her." He couldn't resist. Without waiting to pray, he took a huge bite of the biscuit, and he almost groaned at the pleasure. "These are delicious."

"I know I can go see her without finishing, but I like to reward myself for tasks well done. So if I can get everything finished by the end of the day Thursday, I'll walk over there on Friday. Would you mind if I invited her and Brody to supper Friday night?"

"No, of course not. Do whatever makes you happy." And he'd keep eating her biscuits. He reached for a jar of jam in the middle of the table, something he'd been given by one of his students as a new teacher gift, and he spread it on the biscuit, taking another bite. "Will you promise to make these biscuits for me every day for as long as we're both alive?"

Coral laughed. "I'll make biscuits as often as you like." She took her seat across from him, and reached out to take his hand.

He said a quick prayer for them, and went back to concentrating on his biscuit. "You don't ever have to cook anything else. Just these biscuits."

She tilted her head to one side to study him. "You seem a bit obsessed with the biscuits this morning, Jackson."

"Call me Jack, if you don't mind. That's what my family calls me."

"Jack? I haven't heard anyone else call you that."

He nodded. "As I said, family calls me that. You've never met my family."

"Will I?" she asked.

"Probably. They're not so far away that we can't visit. Maybe during the summer break next year, we can head over."

"All right." She looked down at her food and took a bite of the eggs. "I promise, I won't be cooking eggs for every meal now that I have supplies."

"Do I sound like I'm complaining? These biscuits are incredible!"

Coral laughed at that. "You really are obsessed with the biscuits, aren't you?" She leaned forward as if to impart a great secret. After Jackson—Jack—leaned in to hear it, she whispered, "Wait until you taste my bread."

His eyes widened. "Better than the biscuits?"

She nodded, one corner of her mouth turned up in amusement. "I love to cook!"

"I'm so glad you do!" he said with a smile. "You're not planning on going anywhere, are you? I mean, I really get to keep you?"

"Yes, my cooking is here to stay."

"I don't just want your cooking, Coral. I hope you know that."

She shrugged, looking down at her plate. She knew her value was in what she could do, and not in the person she was. She'd always known that. "All right."

He frowned, realizing that he'd upset her without meaning to. He'd have to find a way to make it up to her. He was just beginning to realize what an incredible woman he'd married, and he hoped he could find a way to make her realize it as well.

After he left for school, Coral got back to work, punching down the bread before starting on the long task of laundry.

It was shortly before eleven when she realized she hadn't sent him off to work with a lunch. She searched until she found a lunch pail, and she cut off two huge slices of the bread she'd made, buttering them with the store-bought butter she'd purchased the day before. She fried up a few pieces of bacon, and added them, before pouring some water into a jar. She added an apple and covered the whole thing with a napkin.

She started on the ten-minute walk to the schoolhouse, thinking about what she'd already done. All of the laundry was on the line, the bread was finished, the walls had been scrubbed. She was ahead of the schedule she'd made for herself, and smiled. She might possibly have some time to do a spot of hunting for supper. She did so prefer fresh meat to meat she'd purchased at the store.

She didn't want to interrupt school, but she didn't want Jack to go hungry, so she went into the coat room at the front of the schoolhouse and peered around the wall, making certain he wasn't in the middle of a lesson.

She smiled when she saw him sitting at his desk, still working on grading the mountain of papers he'd brought home the previous evening, and all the children were working diligently at some task at their desks.

Coral stepped into the classroom, walking up the aisle between the desks to set Jack's lunch on his desk in front of him. "I didn't think to make you a lunch this morning, so I brought it now."

He smiled up at her and nodded. "I've gotten quite used to doing without lunch, so I thank you."

"I'll see you this afternoon." She turned quickly to leave, realizing the eyes of every one of his students were on her.

"Wait a moment." He stood, walking over to her, and putting a casual arm around her shoulders. "Children, I got married on Saturday, and I want to introduce you all to my wife, Coral."

The children all eyed her curiously. "Good morning, children." She had no idea what he wanted her to say, but she was certain that would be appropriate regardless.

The children all chorused back, "Good morning, Mrs. Smythe."

She was startled to hear his last name applied to her, and she looked over at Jackson who looked like he was pleased to hear it. She gave a quick wave to the students, and hurried down the aisle to walk back home.

As she walked, she smiled to herself. He certainly wasn't ashamed of her if he'd introduce his students to her that way. She stepped into the house and grabbed the rifle she had spotted leaning against a corner.

She was back home forty-five minutes later with two rabbits strung over one shoulder. She quickly hung them in the tree to bleed out, her stomach already growling at the notion of rabbit stew for supper.

She buttered a slice of bread for her lunch and sat down for long enough to eat it with a glass of milk, before getting up to scrub the floors. The house would be in perfect shape before the weekend or her name wasn't Coral—Smythe. Her name was Coral Smythe. Why that brought a smile to her lips, she didn't know.

By the time Jack was home from school—and it was hard to think of him as Jack still, but she was determined to do it—she had accomplished everything she'd had on the agenda for the day and then some.

Rabbit stew was simmering on the stove, and she'd baked a spice cake for dessert. She was sitting in a chair beside the table, working on mending the clothes she'd found needed it when she'd done the laundry.

Jack took one step into the house and stopped in his tracks, inhaling deeply. "Something smells delicious."

She smiled. "It's either the rabbit stew I'm cooking, the bread I baked earlier, or the cake I made for dessert."

He sighed happily. "A man could get used to being treated this way!" He looked around the house and noticed all the little things she'd done that day to make it shine. It hadn't been that clean when he'd moved in. "House looks great."

She smiled. "There are still several things I want to get done to it this week, but I'm happy with how it's taking shape."

He put the books, papers, and lunch pail in his hands on the table before sitting down beside her. He waited until she looked up at him before he took the pants she was mending from her hands and put them on the table. Then he took both her hands in his.

"I don't know what I've done to deserve you, but I thank God every day for putting you in my life. I hope you know how much you're already coming to mean to me."

Coral smiled, a distant look in her eyes. "I think you're going to be a much better husband than I thought on that first night."

He grinned. "And I know you'll be a much better wife than I thought that first night."

In response, she stood and got him a small slice of the cake she'd baked with a glass of milk. "I'm sure you're hungry after your long day of work." She sat down and resumed her sewing, her heart sad.

Chapter Six

WHILE JACK GRADED PAPERS that evening, Coral worked diligently at the mending, knowing she could double his wardrobe in a few short hours by fixing a few things. They worked together in companionable silence.

A short while before bed, Jack pushed the papers away. "Would you like to walk with me?"

She looked at him with surprise. "It's almost bedtime."

"Almost, but not yet. Please?"

Coral nodded. "I'd be happy to." She put her mending back into the basket she had appropriated for the task, and placed it in a corner where it wouldn't be in the way. "Let me just grab a shawl. It's getting cool in the evenings."

He waited while she went to their bedroom for her shawl. When she came out, he took it from her and wrapped it around her shoulders before offering her his arm. She took it, surprised that he was acting so cordial with her. She'd expected a lifetime of working together, not a life of courtly manners and gentlemanliness.

Once they were outside, she sighed at the sight of the stars spread overhead. "Why do the stars seem so much brighter in Montana than they did in Massachusetts?"

He grinned. "It's because there's less pollution here. The lower pollution levels make it so we can see the stars better."

"Is that it?" She really hadn't meant for him to answer her question, but having a logical answer was certainly nice. "I'm not as good with astronomy as I am with biology."

"How much do you know about anatomy?" he asked, intrigued.

She smiled. "I was apprenticing under a midwife in Massachusetts without my parents' knowledge. I helped her attend births for several summers before I finished school, and then for the past year."

"Your parents wouldn't have liked that?"

She shook her head. "They didn't like it that I finished school early, either. They felt like a woman's one job in life was to attract a wealthy man to be her husband. I didn't feel called to spend all of my time going to cotillions to try to find someone who would only find fault with me."

"Why would a man have found fault with you?" he asked, surprised by her words.

"Because I overwhelm everyone," she said, her voice small. "What man wants a woman who can do most things better than he can? I'm afraid I can't bring myself to pretend that I can't do a math problem or shoot a rifle, simply to appease the male ego."

He shook his head. "How shallow you make all men out to be."

"Not shallow exactly. Maybe—their egos are easily hurt?"

"Maybe. I'll have you know I'm proud of everything you do so well. I'm amazed by you, Coral."

She shrugged. "Many women can cook. It's not such a wonderful thing."

He nodded. "You're right. Many women can cook. But not many can go out and kill their supper, skin it, and then cook it as if it's nothing. Not many women can do advanced mathematics in their heads without a second thought. I've never met anyone quite like you."

"Are you silently thanking God there's only one of me?" she asked, a twinkle in her eye.

"Well, no, but I'm thanking Him that he gave *me* the only one of you." He stopped walking on the edge of the wooded area not far from his house. "I didn't bring the rifle, so we should probably stay in the open."

She nodded, and turned back toward the house, but his hand on her arm stopped her. "What is it?" she asked.

"Coral, I know you have it in your head that I am only coming to care for you because of your cooking, but I want you to know it's not true. I care for you because of who you are. You are an intelligent, beautiful woman."

"Beautiful? Have you confused me with my sister?" She believed the intelligent part, because she knew she was smart. Beautiful? Not likely.

He shook his head. "Esther's pretty in a different way than you are. To me, Esther is the kind of pretty you look at and walk away from. But you—" He caught her upper arms and pulled her to him. "You're the kind of beauty I want to have in my life and my bed for the rest of my days."

She blushed, happy he couldn't see her clearly in the darkness. She shook her head. "You don't have to say those things to me. I know what I am. I know what I'm not."

"You don't see yourself through my eyes, and I wish for just one moment, you could." His hand stroked her cheek, his thumb coming to rest on her bottom lip and he moved it back and forth, enjoying her soft skin. "May I kiss you, Coral?"

She nodded, her eyes wide. "I'm your wife. You don't even have to ask me that."

"You're my wife, but you're not my love—yet. I want you to be, so I'll ask permission." He lowered his head to hers, kissing her softly, just a touch of his lips against hers. His hands stroked up and down her arms.

Coral gasped against his lips, moving even closer to him. She liked kissing more than a proper woman should, she feared. "Oh, Jack." Her lips parted under his, and she wrapped her arms around his waist, getting as close to him as she could.

After a moment he lifted his head, staring down into her eyes. "I know our marriage started out oddly, but I want your permission to court you. Properly."

She swallowed hard. "To court me? How can you court me when we're already married?"

"I can pay you the same kind of attention I would have done to get to know you better if you'd had the time. May I?"

She nodded, feeling a bit bemused at the prospect. "No one's ever courted me."

"To be quite honest with you, I've never courted anyone either. We'll learn how to do it together."

"You've never courted anyone?" she asked, surprised by his words. "You seem to know what you're doing."

He raised an eyebrow, grinning at her. "I do?"

She shrugged. "Well, I guess you could be fooling me into thinking you know what you're doing, and it would work, because I have no earthly idea how to court someone or to be courted."

He wrapped his arm around her shoulders and walked her back toward the house. "There's a dance at the school on Saturday night."

"There is?"

"Yes. One of my student's father plays the fiddle, and he promised he would play. I'd love to have the honor of your company for the dance, Mrs. Smythe."

She nodded. "Yes, I'd be happy to go with you."

"Good. It's a potluck, so we'll have to take something with us. If you don't mind, I think it would be best if you were the one to see to that and not me."

"Absolutely. I'll make something for it. Do you know if they need items for the actual meal or desserts more?"

"No idea."

"Maybe I'll do one of each." As embarrassed as she was that she was so good at everything, she felt the need to show off her skills as a wife. She always had.

Jack smiled, keeping his arm firmly around her. "Whatever you think is best."

"I wonder if Esther and Brody know about the dance?"

"If they don't, it might be nice if you told them."

"I'll do that. I should be able to go see her on Friday without a problem."

"Good. I really am impressed with all you've gotten done so quickly at home."

"I'm glad you're pleased with it." When they arrived at the house, she stepped inside, while he stayed back. "I'll stay out here for twenty minutes to give you time to get ready."

Coral looked at Jack and stood on her tiptoes to brush her lips across his. "Thank you for caring about my feelings so much. I appreciate it."

He smiled, stroking his hand down her back. "You're special, Coral."

She turned and hurried to get ready, not answering him. She was starting to believe that he truly thought she was special. She didn't know how, and she didn't know why, but maybe if she was special in his eyes, he really would keep her forever.

She was already under the covers when he came into bed a short while later. She normally fell asleep the moment her head hit the pillow, but for some reason she was restless that night, thinking about their walk and his desire to court her.

She kept her eyes closed until she felt the mattress dip beside her. "Why have you never courted a girl?"

Jack turned on his side facing her, something he'd never done before. Usually as soon as they were in bed together, they would lay stiff as boards, pretending the other wasn't there. "There was a girl I wanted to court when I was still living on my step-dad's farm. She was the daughter of a neighboring farmer, and she was pretty as a picture."

When he said the girl was pretty, Coral's heart drooped. So he wanted a pretty girl. "Did you ask if you could court her?"

"I did. I went to her pa to ask him first, knowing it was proper. And then I went to her and asked."

"What did she say?"

"She told me that she wouldn't spend the rest of her life tied to a farmer. She'd seen the hardship her parents went through, relying on the seasons and the rainfall as they did. She wouldn't be any part of it." He sighed. "So I went off to school to be a teacher, thinking that she would be happier with that."

"What happened then?"

"When I came home with my new teaching certificate, ready to teach in the school we'd both attended, I found out she'd married a local farmer."

Coral turned to face him on the bed, taking one of his hands that rested atop the covers in hers. "I'd say I'm sorry, but I'm not. If she hadn't done that, maybe you'd have married her. And where would I be?"

He smiled at that, bringing the hand in is to his lips. "I really don't know, but I'm sure the answer would not be in my bed. And that would be truly dreadful, wouldn't it?"

Coral blushed, glad the room was dark. "I don't think a man should be talking to the woman he's courting that way."

"Oh, but when we're in bed together, we're no longer just courting, Coral. When we're in bed together, we're husband and wife."

"Do you regret promising to wait until I turn eighteen?"

"Sometimes," he answered honestly. "But I do think it's smart for both of us. We'll have plenty of time to get to know each other and know our own hearts if we wait." He kissed her softly before rolling onto his back. "Now go to sleep."

Coral grinned, rolling to her side facing away from him so he wouldn't see how happy he had made her with his words. "G'night, Jack."

"Good night, Coral."

Chapter Seven

IT WASN'T LONG BEFORE Coral had the house exactly as she wanted it. All the windows had been scrubbed clean, and there were new curtains hanging from them. On Friday morning, she made lunch for Jack and sent him off to school, and then she did the breakfast dishes before walking over to see Esther.

It was a longer walk than she'd realized, and it made her wish she'd ridden over, but she didn't mind too terribly much. It gave her time to think about her marriage and Jack's proposition to her.

The night before he'd come home with flowers in his hand, a sweet gesture. She had fussed over the flowers and tucked them into a glass to put in the center of the table. She had found poems written out in his hand throughout the house. Not poems he had written, of course, but poems he had taken the time to copy from some of the great poets. She was starting to feel like he really might care for her.

When she finally reached her sister's house, she knocked on the door, hoping Esther hadn't left for the day. Her sister opened the door wide and cried out as she grabbed her in a hug. "You're just the person I needed to see today!"

Coral smiled. "What can I help you with?"

"It's not just that I need help with something, you know. I'm genuinely happy to see you." Esther waved her hand toward the table. "Sit! Sit!"

Coral took a seat, and smiled at her sister, who looked slightly frazzled. "Is marriage easier with me gone?" she asked softly.

Esther sighed, sitting down across from her sister. "I hope we didn't make you feel unwelcome."

Coral shrugged. "I understood why you didn't want me here. I don't know how my marriage would be if you were living with me." She smiled, letting Esther know she really did understand the problems she'd caused.

"How is marriage for you? Is he a good man?"

Coral nodded emphatically. "A very good man. He actually seems to like my—strangeness."

"Your strangeness? Don't speak in riddles, Coral. I always get confused when you do that."

Coral wanted to laugh. She hadn't seen Esther in a week and it was as if they'd only been apart five minutes. "I'm sorry. He likes it that I'm good at—so many things."

Esther rolled her eyes. "That you're good at everything, you mean? You scare me sometimes. I'm glad you've always been on my side, because I really wouldn't want you for an enemy."

Coral bit her lip to keep from laughing at her sister's words. Jack's easy acceptance of what she considered her greatest weakness helped her see the humor in other people's fear of her. "Why were you so glad to see me this morning?"

Esther sighed. "I was trying to bake a cake. I've thrown out four already. I'm going to go through all the sugar and flour we have trying to make one dessert for my husband."

"I can help you with that. You should have just come over to get help."

Esther nodded. "I had decided to try once more, and if that didn't work, I was going to march right down to that house of yours and beg for your help."

"I came to invite you and Brody for supper tonight," Coral said as she walked to the work table.

Esther seemed to consider for a moment, but then she shook her head. "I do appreciate the offer, Coral, but not tonight. I want to cook a special meal for Brody tonight."

Coral shrugged. "All right. What kind of cake are you trying to make?" Esther pointed to the recipe on the counter, and Coral walked over to look at it. "Let's do it then."

Coral spent the next hour showing her sister how to make a cake step-by-step. When they removed it from the oven, Esther's face lit up. "It's beautiful! Will it taste good?"

"Of course, it will. Best cake you've ever eaten. I promise."

"I believe you!"

"Are you and Brody going to the dance at the schoolhouse tomorrow night?" Coral asked.

"I didn't realize there was a dance. Oh, that sounds wonderful!"

"So you'll go?" Coral was almost desperate for her sister to be there, so she'd know at least one person other than Jack. Her husband would be called away from her to say the prayer over the meal and do other host-type things, and she wanted to have someone there she could talk to comfortably.

Esther nodded. "I don't know if Brody knows about it, but I promise you, we'll be there. I couldn't pass up the chance to go to a dance. I haven't done anything social at all since we left Massachusetts. I feel like I may have forgotten how to waltz already!"

Coral wanted to laugh at her sister's lament. "I promise you haven't forgotten how to dance. Even I remember how, and I never put those lessons to good use."

"You should have allowed one of the young men back in Massachusetts to court you."

"No one ever asked."

"Because they were afraid of you! To keep a man, you have to show him that you're not better at everything than he is." Esther shook her head. "I've been telling you the same thing for years. You have to pretend to be inept at least once in a while, so a man won't feel overwhelmed by you."

"No, I really don't have to do that," Coral insisted. "Jack likes me just as I am."

"Jack, is it? Brody always refers to him as Jackson."

"He's asked me to call him Jack."

Esther took her sister's hand. "He's kind to you? He doesn't hurt you?"

Coral's face transformed into a grin. "He's kinder to me than I ever dreamed imaginable. He's a good, caring man. I needed him in my life."

"I've been worried about you, and I wanted to go see you on Monday, but Brody told me not to interfere."

"I promise you, he's wonderful. He treats me like I'm someone very special."

"You *are* someone special." Esther stood up and walked to the work table. "I need to make lunch for Brody. Any suggestions?"

Coral smiled, shaking her head at her sister. "Do you want me to make lunch?"

"That would be wonderful, if you don't mind."

"I don't." While Esther watched, Coral fixed lunch for the couple.

"Are you sure you're making enough?" Esther asked.

"It's just the two of you."

"But you can't make lunch and then run off. I'll feel guilty."

"No need. I want to see if I can do a bit of hunting before dinner," Coral explained. "It would be nice if I could make a good venison steak, and then I'd have meat to dry for the winter."

"But how would you get the deer home if you were able to shoot it?" Esther asked practically.

"I'd gut it right there in the woods and make it lighter, and then I'd drag it back. Trust me, I'm capable."

"There's nothing you can't do. Trust me. I remember."

Coral shrugged. "I'm not ashamed of it anymore."

"Why would you *ever* be ashamed of it?"

"You were telling me to hide it from a man just a short while ago. You must think I should be ashamed."

Esther stared at her sister, astonishment clear on her face. "Oh no, Coral. That's never what I meant at all. I was never meaning to tell you that you shouldn't be so good at everything. Just that we all need to play these little games with men so they think they're better than us. See the difference?"

"Not at all. It's fine, though. I'm not ashamed, and I won't be again. Jack has helped me to see that how I am is really a good thing. He calls me his marvel."

"I'm so glad he's giving you the confidence you should have always had." Esther grabbed her sister in a spontaneous hug. "You deserve to be happy."

Coral kept those words in mind as she walked home to get the rifle. She did deserve to be happy. She wasn't at fault for her mother becoming a recluse. Her birth mother and her father had been at fault for that. She hadn't caused her birth, and she couldn't control the circumstances of them. So therefore, she shouldn't be forced to spend the rest of her life repenting for other people's actions.

JACK WAS OUTSIDE WITH the children for their lunch break when he heard the rifle. He smiled, wondering what fabulous meal Coral would be making that evening. Had she found the latest poem he'd left for her? She hadn't commented on them, but the night before, she'd walked around the house with a dreamy look on her face, and when he'd pulled her to him to kiss her goodnight, she'd gone willingly into his arms.

He still couldn't believe his luck. With as many bachelors as there were in the area, she'd chosen *him*. He didn't deserve to have her, but he was glad he did. All he had to do was wait a little longer for her to turn eighteen. Every day since he'd made that deal with her, he'd regretted it. She was worth waiting for though.

As he walked home, he looked around for fresh flowers to replace the ones gracing their table. She deserved to always have something new and pretty around her.

Every day, she seemed to spend a little more time on her appearance, and she seemed to get prettier and prettier. He didn't know if his feelings were just growing so she seemed prettier to him, but he didn't think that was it at all.

She truly was doing something that made her prettier. He hadn't been sure how he felt about her hair when he'd first seen her. He'd always liked a true deep red-head, but her hair was more the orange of a carrot. Now, every day she pulled her hair back in a becoming style, and he realized that her hair was a part of her beauty. She may not be beautiful to other men, but to him, she was one of the loveliest women he'd ever seen.

When he walked through the door, he saw her sitting at the table, carefully mending a tear in a pair of his pants. She was willing to work hard to make certain he didn't have to waste a dime of his hard-earned money. She never asked him to buy her anything, except supplies, so she could make his meals.

He took the pants from her and set them on the table, and then he took her hand, pulling her to her feet. "I've missed you today," he said, handing her the flowers he'd picked.

She took the flowers and buried her face in them. "They're lovely."

"Not half as lovely as you." He pulled her to him, kissing her softly. "Did you have a good day?"

She nodded. "Esther had supper plans already, so they're not coming tonight, but they'll be at the dance tomorrow."

"At least you'll get to see her there."

"She said something that made me wonder today."

Jack pulled back, looking at her. "I hope she didn't make you feel like you're doing something wrong." He barely knew Esther, but he felt like the majority of Coral's insecurities came from her sister.

Coral shook her head. "No, not at all. But she told me that the reason none of the men in Massachusetts wanted to court me is because I am too good at everything. And that I should have pretended to be bad at things, so men could feel superior."

He laughed. "A lot of men probably would have preferred if you did that."

"But not you?"

"Not me. Why should you pretend to not be good at something? There's no point. I have a woman who can conquer the world with one hand tied behind her back. What's wrong with that?"

Coral buried her face in the front of his shirt. "Not one little thing."

Chapter Eight

AFTER SUPPER, JACK looked at his wife with a look of pure admiration. "This meal was amazing."

Coral smiled. "I'm glad you enjoyed it." She'd made venison steak and paired it with baked potatoes and fresh bread. "What do you think I should make for the dance tomorrow? I could do just some bread or biscuits and a cake? Or would you prefer I made a full meal?"

He grinned. "Truthfully, I'd rather never eat another person's cooking as long as I live. Why didn't you tell me you were such an amazing cook?"

She looked over her shoulder at him with a laugh. "Jack, I did! You told me no one can be good at everything. Remember?"

"I do remember. I really didn't think it was possible." He shook his head. "I guess I've been proven wrong."

She laughed. "Well, at least I can safely say I wasn't overstating how well I do things."

"You truly are a marvel." He got up and walked over to a small table where he'd put his papers to grade when he'd come in that afternoon. "I am still not entirely caught up on grading papers after taking the weekend off. I'm afraid I'll be working all evening again."

"Do you want my help again? I'm always willing."

"You do so much! I hate to ask you to spend your time helping me with my work."

Coral shrugged. "We're married, and I truly believe a woman should be a helper to her man. I'm more than willing to do it."

He finally nodded. "I'd like that."

She smiled. "Let me just finish the dishes, and I'll be ready."

Fifteen minutes later, she brought over a big plate of cookies, two saucers, and two glasses of milk. "I thought we might enjoy a snack while we work on the papers."

Jack took a cookie and placed it on the saucer. "Thank you. I appreciate you always thinking of me."

Coral smiled. "I'm your wife. It's my job to think of the little comforts."

He shook his head at her. "I hope you know that you don't have to. I do understand how busy you are during the day."

She chuckled at that. "Perhaps I will be once the children start coming along, but for now, I'm not busy at all. I've caught up on the housework. I'm working on sewing some curtains, but once I'm done with that, I'll have nothing to do but cook and keep things clean, which is easy now that the house is already there."

"You weren't raised for this kind of work. I'm always amazed at how you seem to have taken to it."

"I may not have been raised for hard work, but I was never meant to sit around doing nothing. My parents accepted that early on, and they learned not to ask how I kept myself busy. They hated the time I spent in the kitchen, learning to cook and bake, but I enjoyed it so much. The cook was really like a second mother to me."

"When I was young, before my father died, we had money. We lived in a fancy house, back in New York, and my mother sat around doing nothing but embroidering. She was miserable. My father was given to drink, and he wasn't a kind man." He took the math papers from the stack in front of him and put them in a pile in front of her. "She remarried soon after he died to a good man. She had a hard time getting used to doing the household chores, though. They were foreign to her. She had to learn to cook, and she hated it."

"I see. So were you expecting me to be like your mother?"

He shrugged. "I really didn't know what to expect, but I thought it was a possibility."

Coral reached out and took his hand in hers. "I genuinely enjoy sewing. I'm not fond of scrubbing floors, but I don't know of a single woman who is. I will do whatever is required of me as your wife, and I'll do it with a smile on my face. I've chosen to marry you and to live this life with you. It's up to me to choose to be happy in it."

"Are you certain you're only seventeen?" Truly, he had never expected that much wisdom from a girl of her age.

She nodded. "That's what my parents tell me anyway."

"When exactly is your birthday?" He tried to keep his voice casual with the question, but he was sure she'd understand why he was asking.

"November first."

"So it's not two months away. It's more like four and a half weeks away. It's already the end of September."

She nodded, blushing as she pulled the papers toward her. "Yes."

He changed the subject, seeing that the topic embarrassed her. He loved that she blushed, but he loved everything about her. A week before he'd have scoffed at the notion that he could fall in love with this young, headstrong woman, but there was something terribly special about her. He just hoped he could find a way to convince her to trust him with her heart.

CORAL TOOK HIM AT HIS word the next day, fixing venison stew to take to the dance, as well as bread, and two dozen cookies for dessert. She knew it was too much to take, but she didn't care. If Jack only wanted to eat her cooking, then he had that right.

He spent the day at the table, finishing up the paper grading that needed to be done, while she first cooked, and then joined him at the table. "Do you want help grading papers?"

He shook his head. "No, I'm working on essays now. There's really no way someone else could grade them."

She pulled out one of her anatomy books instead. "I'll just study then." She flipped to the page she had last been working on back in Massachusetts, and pored over the book.

Jack watched her for a few minutes, noting how quickly she flipped the pages. It was as if she was looking at the pictures and turning to the next page without actually reading the words. There was no way she could possibly be retaining anything.

Coral looked up, realizing he was watching her. "What?"

"You're not actually reading the words."

She sighed. "Yes, I am."

"How can you be? You're spending mere seconds on each page." He'd never seen anyone read with anything approaching the speed she was reading.

She frowned. "I thought you were used to me."

"What does that even mean?"

She turned the book back two pages before pushing it across the table to him. "Start reading in the top left hand corner of the page," she instructed him.

He gave her a perplexed look before looking down at the page. Coral closed her eyes and recited the first paragraph to him—without missing a single word. "How?" It was one simple word, but there was a great deal of emotion in it.

She shrugged, taking the book back from him. "I don't know. I wish I did. I've been able to do that since I was a little girl." She looked down at her hands, wishing she had an explanation. "I showed my mother when I first started school. I thought it was a good thing." She shook her head. "The look of horror on her face will stay with me forever. I've never shown anyone else, and I don't think Mama ever really believed what she saw."

"That's incredible. I—I've never seen anything like it."

"I can do it with other things too. It's like I can see something done once, and I will remember how to do it forever. I don't tell people, because I don't want them to think there's something wrong with me."

"There's nothing wrong with you." Jack took her hand in his. "Truly, you are an amazing woman. I knew it a week ago, but now, watching that—I don't even know what to say."

"I love being able to learn so much so quickly, but I hate not being able to show that I have knowledge. I have to hide, so people don't lock me away somewhere."

"Lock you away?"

She shrugged. "I've always had in my head that if people found out how easily and quickly I learned things, they would lock me in an asylum."

Jack shook his head at her. "No, but they might lock you in a laboratory and study you."

"I don't want that either! I want to live a normal life. Well, I want to be a doctor, but I'd settle for being a midwife. I'd be a good one."

"You would. There's no doubt in my mind. Is that why you continue to study the medical books?"

She shrugged. "I need something to do. I go crazy just sitting around. I thought about adding on a room to the house, but I wasn't sure what you'd think of that, so I will just study the medical textbooks I brought with me."

He looked at her as if seeing her for the first time. "Do you think you could add a room onto the house?"

She nodded. "I have no doubt. I read how to build a house in a book once. I'm sure adding a room on wouldn't be much different."

"I have science books, and literature books, and poetry books. They're all in a trunk in the bedroom. Please feel free to read through it if you run out of other things to read."

"You don't mind?" She was still half-afraid he'd reject her, knowing her deepest darkest secret.

He shook his head. "I think it's wonderful that you want to keep learning. I want to see you excel at everything, and you already do!"

She smiled at that. "Not at everything."

"I thought you said you were good at everything," he said with a wink.

"I'm not good at people," she admitted, her voice soft. "I don't know how to relate. I even frighten my own sister sometimes. Oh, she doesn't tell me that, but I can tell. It's all over her face."

"Esther has never seen you do what you just did for me? You're sure?"

Coral nodded. "I'm positive. I've been so careful to hide it. But she's still seen me shoot a gun into the center of a target the first time I picked one up. She's seen me do so many things that seem impossible."

"But they *are* possible. You do them."

She nodded. "I just wish I knew why and how."

"The why is because you're brilliant. The how? I guess because you were born that way. As far as I'm concerned there need be no further explanation." He sighed. "You probably shouldn't let anyone else see it though. I'm afraid you're right about how afraid people would be."

"Because they're afraid I'll try to take over the world?"

"Not at all. Because they're afraid you would succeed without trying." He brought her hand to his lips. "I need to work on these essays now. Please, continue glancing at the pages so you can memorize them. I don't think anyone would object to having a skilled healer in the community. Even one who didn't have the formal training to go with it."

"Thank you."

"Why are you thanking me?"

"Because you're accepting me for who I am. That means so much."

He smiled. "I always will. Never be afraid to share your secrets with me."

Chapter Nine

AT THE DANCE, CORAL felt extremely shy. She'd never enjoyed being around huge crowds of people like her sister did. She stayed close to Jack's side and met the parents of his students.

"Mrs. Sanford, this is my wife, Coral."

Coral smiled, holding her hand out to the older woman. "It's so nice to meet you, Mrs. Sanford."

"We had no idea our dear teacher was even courting anyone, but we're happy to welcome you to our community, Mrs. Smythe."

"I'm happy to be here." Coral hoped the woman would move on, because she had absolutely nothing to say to her.

"Where are you from?" Mrs. Sanford asked.

"I lived in Massachusetts until just recently." *Please walk away. Please walk away.*

"Wow. That's far away! Are you any relation to Mrs. Finnegan?"

Coral should have known Esther would already have met at least half the community. She was so outgoing. What Coral wouldn't give for just a bit of that now. "Yes, she's my sister."

Mrs. Sanford's brows drew together, and Coral could read her mind. *They don't look like sisters.*

"I see." Mrs. Sanford took her leave then, and Coral sighed heavily.

"What's wrong?" Jack asked, his hand going to the small of her back.

"I'm being compared to Esther again and found lacking."

"That's because they've never seen you do mathematics in your head. Or seen you barely glance at a page before memorizing it. If they could see those things, they'd be impressed."

"And shocked and frightened..." Coral couldn't believe it when a giggle escaped her. She was making fun of how different she was, and she didn't think she'd ever been able to do that before.

Jack laughed, the sound loud and booming, causing everyone to turn and look their way. Several of the men gave approving nods.

Esther entered the schoolhouse then, and sashayed across the room. Coral couldn't believe just how much her sister filled up a room. She stopped to talk to everyone as she walked through the small building. All of the desks had been taken outside for the evening, and would be returned after the party.

Coral leaned over and whispered to Jack, "I wish I could be half as likable as she is. She has everyone in the room eating out of the palm of her hand, and she just arrived."

"You're not jealous of your sister, are you?"

"Only a lot." She put on a brave face as Esther made her way over to her. "I'm glad you were able to make it."

Esther smiled, reaching out to hug her sister. "Of course, I made it. I wouldn't miss this for anything." She was wearing her prettiest dress, a pink silk gown with an embroidered bodice. The only woman in the room wearing gloves, she should have looked odd, but instead, she made every other woman in the room look positively dowdy.

"Where's Brody?" Jack asked, not able to stop himself from comparing the sisters. The first time he'd seen them together, his wife had been the loser in the comparison. This time, though, he could see the inner beauty his wife displayed. Her sister was kind enough, but she didn't glow from within the way Coral did.

"He's seeing to the horses."

"You brought the wagon?" Coral asked, without thinking first. Of course they brought the wagon. Her sister wouldn't dream of walking all that way, dancing the night away, and then walking home again.

"I didn't want to mess up my gown by walking," Esther said, as if her sister should have known that's what she was thinking.

"Of course not."

Jack smiled at Esther. "It's good to see you again."

Esther nodded at her new brother-in-law. "And you. I hope you're taking good care of my baby sister."

"It's my job. And she's taking good care of me as well."

"I'm sure she is. Brody is missing her cooking already."

"You're welcome to come to our place for supper any time." He made the offer automatically, hoping she wouldn't take him up on it. He knew Esther was a lot of the reason Coral thought so little of herself.

"Thank you." Esther turned toward the door, her eyes catching Brody. "There's my man."

Brody was in the doorway, and his eyes were scanning the room. When they lit on Esther, he walked toward her as if pulled her way by a magnet. When he'd reached his wife, his arm went about her shoulders, anchoring her to his side.

Brody's eyes met Jackson's. "How's married life, Mr. Smythe?"

Jack smiled. "I couldn't have asked for a more beautiful, sweet woman. I'm thrilled with married life."

Brody looked surprised. "You are?" He looked back and forth between Coral and Jackson. "Of course you are. Coral's an excellent cook."

"She is. She's wonderful at so many things, isn't she? I just thank God every day that she chose *me*."

Brody seemed to want to argue with Jack's version of events, but he didn't. "You are a fortunate man."

Jack nodded. "That I am." He kissed Coral's cheek. "I need to say the blessing, and then we'll eat." He looked at Esther. "Did you put your dish on the table?"

"Oh, I knew Coral would make enough for both of us."

Jack blinked for a moment, having a hard time believing that she'd said that. She was right though. "Yes, she made enough for several households. Excuse me, I'll say the prayer."

Coral watched him as he said the prayer and then led the way to the food table. He not only filled a plate for himself, but he filled one for her as well. Coral was thankful. They stood around eating while holding their plates in their hands. "I got a big portion of your stew," Jack told Coral. "It's delicious as always."

After they'd eaten, it was time for the dance, and Coral realized that other than her debutante ball, she hadn't danced with a man. When Jack took her into his arms and slowly began to twirl her around the room, she felt like she was dancing on air. He was a good dancer, guiding her through the steps seamlessly.

"Where did you learn to dance so well?" she asked.

"My mother. She hated that I wasn't getting the kind of upbringing I'd been born for, so she would dance with me in the evenings, so I could return to the life I'd had to leave when she married my step-father."

"I don't understand. How could you return to it?"

"My grandparents would have taken us in, and did for a short time before she decided to remarry. I always had an open invitation to go back East and take up the reins of my grandfather's business."

"What did he do?" she asked.

"He owned a bank."

"And you didn't want to do that?"

He shook his head emphatically. "My grandfather disapproved of my step-father, and I felt like he treated him unfairly. Although his mistreatment didn't extend to me, I had no desire to be part of the lifestyle that led people to look down on others. We're all equal."

She smiled and nodded. "I agree. Wholeheartedly."

After the dance was over, he and some of the other men put the desks back into the schoolhouse, and Coral was pleased to see that Brody was one of the men who helped. Esther stood beside her, yawning.

"You seem very tired tonight," Coral said.

Esther shrugged. "I'm not used to all the physical labor. I'll get to where I'm good at it though. Brody is worth that to me."

When the men had finished, the sisters said goodnight with hugs and Coral set off with Jack toward their home. "That went better than I expected," she told him.

"You didn't expect it to go well?"

She shrugged. "I really don't do well with people. I know you don't believe me, but I tend to be prickly because I get so overwhelmed."

"Like you were the night we met?" he asked, finally understanding why she'd seemed to be a different person the night he'd met her.

"Exactly! I don't know why you agreed to marry me."

"I was very nervous, and you agreed to cook all my meals."

She laughed. "I always knew you had only one thing on your mind when you married me."

He shrugged. "I don't deny it. And I have to say, you've fulfilled that duty admirably. Now I have something entirely different on my mind, but that will still have to wait."

She turned her head to him, a slight grin on her face. "We'll know each other so much better in a month. Don't you think this period of getting to know who we are without the marriage bed interfering is good for us?"

"You know, I really do. Most of the time. But sometimes, I just want to have my way with you."

She laughed. "You make it sound positively naughty, Mr. Smythe."

He wrapped his arm around her waist and pulled her closer to him. "Not when it's between married people."

She sighed contentedly. "Thank you for being so attentive this evening. I think Esther was worried about me until she saw us together."

"And she's not worried any longer?"

"She doesn't seem to be. She seems to be surprised that we genuinely like each other, but she no longer is worried."

"That's a good thing, I guess."

"Oh, it surely is." She thought of something she'd been wanting to mention. "Is it possible for us to get a dog or a cat? I spend so many hours alone that I feel like an animal would be the perfect companion."

He thought about it for a moment. "Why don't I ask around and see if anyone has a new litter they're trying to get rid of. I wouldn't mind having an animal around either." He opened the door to the house and let her precede him inside. "Do you have a preference of a dog or a cat?"

She shrugged. "I'd prefer a dog, but a cat would be helpful with rodents." She'd seen mice in the house a few times and would be glad to get rid of them.

"So you'd be happy with either?"

She nodded. "I want a dog, but I can see the benefits of a cat."

"I'll see what I can do to make that happen." He yawned widely. "It's been a long day. Are you ready for bed?"

She nodded. "Just give me five minutes."

"Are you certain that's long enough?" He'd gotten into the habit of giving her exactly twenty minutes every night.

"I might still be braiding my hair when you come in, but if that won't bother you, five minutes is enough."

"I'll see you in five minutes then." He leaned down to kiss her cheek before heading outside.

As he wandered, he thought about how uncomfortable she'd truly been that night, and he realized something about her. She was much more at home with books than she ever would be with people. It wasn't a criticism, of course, because he understood the feeling completely. For the most part, he felt exactly the same way.

He'd rather be with books than anyone else in the world. Except for her, of course. In just one short week, his Coral had managed to worm her way into his heart. He loved her.

He knew then he wanted to find a special way to tell her. Something that would make her realize that he accepted everything about her, and not just the parts that he liked. It would have to be a grand gesture of some sort, and it would take some planning. He'd do it though, because she mattered so much to him.

Chapter Ten

THE NEXT MONTH FLEW by, with Coral getting to know Jack a bit better every day. On the eve of her birthday, she sat with him in front of the warm stove. He was grading papers while she read one of her anatomy books. "This is my last book," she said. She wanted to ask for more, but she knew they really didn't have the money.

He sighed. "And there's no point in your trying to re-read anything because you have it all memorized still." He reached out and took her hand. "I do wish I could buy you a whole library of books."

"I know. I'm just going to need a new project to keep me busy for a while." She looked out the window, watching the snow fall. "This is going to be a very long winter if I'm home all the time with nothing to do."

"I know you were collecting some scraps of cloth. Do you have enough to make a quilt?"

"I do, and I'll start on one tomorrow." It wouldn't take her nearly long enough, but she could stay occupied for a while with it.

"Will you have time to bake a cake tomorrow?" he asked.

She shrugged. "Sure, I can do that. Nothing else to do."

He patted her hand and went back to grading the papers in front of him. He wanted to finish them, so he'd have the weekend free. He wanted to tell her about his birthday surprise for her, but he wasn't going to spoil it. He'd worked too hard to get everything just right without her knowing.

WHEN CORAL WOKE THE following morning, she stretched and rolled over. She loved to see Jack's head on the pillow beside hers every morning. She sat straight up in bed when she realized he wasn't lying beside her. Where could he be? In all their weeks of being married, he'd never woken up before she did.

She rolled from the bed, shivering and grabbed her wrapper, pulling it over her shoulders. Opening the bedroom door, she peeked out and saw Jack on one knee in front of the stove, starting a fire.

"What are you doing up so early?" she asked.

He sighed. He'd slept too late for the first part of her surprise. Without answering, he finished lighting the fire and then stood up. "I wanted to make breakfast for you for a change. For your birthday."

She frowned. "It's not my birthday. Not for another week."

He grinned. "Did you lose track of the days? It's November first. Happy birthday, Coral." He walked to her and pulled her into his arms, kissing her sweetly.

She wrapped her arms around his neck, smiling up at him. "Well, I'm glad you remembered, because I seem to have forgotten."

"Well, you sit down, and I'll make you some breakfast."

She watched him for a moment as he got down a pan and cut off some pieces of bacon, putting them into the cold iron skillet without even heating it first. "You know what, Jack? I know how much you hate to cook. I'll do it."

He looked at her over his shoulder. "I wanted to make your birthday morning special for you."

"You already have, just by remembering." She took the skillet from him and removed the bacon, then put the pan on the stove to heat it.

"I was supposed to heat the pan first?" he asked, watching her carefully. He wanted to be able to at least make breakfast sometimes.

She nodded. "The bacon will be crispier that way." She broke the eggs into a bowl and added a dollop of milk before using a fork to mix them, holding the bowl against her belly.

"You look beautiful this morning, Coral."

She looked at him with wide eyes. "You don't have to tell me that. I know I'm not a beauty."

"I disagree. The more I know you, the more beautiful I realize you are. It's like there's something inside you that just radiates goodness and beauty."

"Have you been reading more love poems?"

He shook his head. "I haven't. Those were my own words." He watched as she removed the bacon from the pan and poured out some of the grease before adding the egg mixture. "Have you enjoyed the poems?"

Coral blushed and nodded. "I've kept every one of them."

"Have you now? Why didn't you say anything about them?" He'd left her at least one poem a day in various places around the house for her to find.

"I—well, I didn't know what to say. No one has ever tried to woo me before."

"Is it working?"

"Is what working?"

"My efforts to woo you. Are they working?"

She nodded slowly as she stirred the eggs, not looking at him. "You're awfully good at it."

He smiled at that, pleased she'd been happy with his efforts. "I'm glad you think so. I'm not so certain myself."

"Why not?"

He shrugged. "Well, I still don't know where I stand with my own wife. You'd think if I was good at wooing, I'd at least know how she felt about me."

"I—I don't know what to say to that." She knew she loved him, but she wasn't sure she was ready to give him that kind of power over her. What if he didn't love her back? Then she'd be crushed.

He walked up behind her and wrapped his arms around her waist, resting his cheek atop her head. "You don't have to say anything just yet."

"But I have to say something later?"

He shrugged. "I can't *ever* force you to say anything. I hope you'll *want* to say something."

She carefully removed the skillet from the top of the stove and rested it on a potholder before turning in his arms. She was very aware that now she was eighteen all their agreements were over, and he could start asking for more from her any time he wanted. "I think you're an amazing husband."

He smiled, stroking her cheek. "That'll do to begin with."

She stood on tiptoe and kissed him softly before turning back to the food she'd prepared. "Sit down, and I'll serve this."

He shook his head. "No, you sit down and I'll serve, and I'm cleaning up afterward. Maybe I can't cook, but I know how to put food on a plate and wash a few dishes."

"Are you sure?" She felt like she was doing something wrong by letting him serve her. It was supposed to be the other way around.

He nodded. "I'm positive. Sit." He scooped the eggs onto two plates and added bacon while she made her way to the table. Then he took the toast she'd prepared from the oven and slathered it with butter, adding two pieces to each plate. Carrying them to the table, he asked, "Do you want coffee?"

"Yes, please."

She waited as he got coffee and forks for both of them and sat across from her. Taking her hand, he blessed their meal. "I'm sorry I didn't have time to make breakfast before you got up like I'd planned."

"I really appreciate the thought, and it'll be nice not to have to do the dishes for a change."

While Jack did the dishes, Coral went into the bedroom to dress for the day. She wondered what else her new husband had in store for her, because it was apparent he'd thought about this day a great deal.

When she stepped into the main room, she saw that he was just putting the last of the dishes on the shelf. "Thank you for doing the dishes for me, Jack. It's a perfect birthday present."

Jack turned to her and smiled. "Do you want to bake the cake now? And I can give you your presents at lunchtime?"

"Presents? When did you have time to get me a present?" She was surprised he'd even thought of anything. She walked to him and wrapped her arms around his neck, pulling his head down for a kiss. "You're the best husband in the whole world. You know that?"

"You don't even know what I got you yet! What if I got you some new linens so you can make me underwear? Or some yarn so you can make me socks?"

"Then I'll thank you kindly for giving me something to do to get me through the longer winter months."

He shook his head. "Well, I should have thought of those things then!"

She smiled, enjoying his playfulness. So often he was serious, and she loved it when he showed this side of himself. "Whatever it is, I will be thankful that you even remembered my birthday."

"How could I forget?" He looked into her eyes, making it clear that he remembered very well what his promise to her had been. "This is a date that I have had in my mind for a good while now."

She blushed. "Well, it's finally here."

"Bake the cake. I have just a few more papers to grade while you do, and then I can take the rest of the weekend off to be with you."

She smiled at that. "All right. I'll get to it right now."

"Stay out of the bedroom for the rest of the day, will you?"

"What?" She turned to him. "What are you doing back there?"

He shrugged, a huge grin on his face. "Just stay out until I say you can go in."

"Whatever you say." Coral turned away, unable to stifle the smile that spread across her face. He had an air of secrecy about him that was a lot of fun for her.

She started by baking some bread, so they'd have enough to make it through the weekend and then used some of the venison she'd shot the day before to make another stew. Venison stew was his favorite meal, so she did her best to make it as much as she could. She'd started curing the hides of the animals as well, knowing they would be able to sell them eventually.

She baked gingerbread, knowing it was his favorite and topped it with whipped cream. He stayed back in the bedroom, and a couple of times she heard him grunting, as if he was doing something hard. She heard hammering as well and wondered what on earth the man was doing in there.

Finally, it was time for lunch, and she called to him. "Jack? It's time for lunch. Are you finished?"

"I'll be right out." Jack slipped through a very narrow opening in the door, not trusting her not to look. "I'm finished, but you still don't get to go in there until after we've had our cake, and I've washed the lunch dishes."

She sighed. "I'm going to die of curiosity!"

He shrugged. "Patience is a virtue. Don't you want to be virtuous?"

"Not particularly." Usually, she did, but right that second, she just wanted to see what he'd been working on.

He caught her arm and turned her toward the table. "Eat first."

"Fine." She sat down at the table she'd already set and waited for him to take his spot. After their prayer, she started asking him questions. "Can you give me just one hint?"

"You'll like it."

"That's not a hint! I want a *real* hint!"

"Coral, you'll never get to see it if you don't hurry and eat." Truthfully, he was impatient as well. He'd been working on her birthday surprise for over a month, and he couldn't wait for her to see what he'd done.

Coral ate quickly, wanting to know right away. She'd never been so impatient to see what a surprise was in her entire life. When she was finished, she sat back and patted her stomach. "I don't think I'm hungry enough for cake."

He frowned. "I guess we'll wait until you get hungry enough for cake for your surprise then."

She glared at him. "Fine. I'll get us both some cake."

"I'll get the cake. You sit here."

Instead of obeying Jack, she jumped up and put the dishes in the basin. She'd already started the hot water boiling so the dishes could be done immediately.

Jack got them each a piece of the gingerbread and a glass of milk. "I said to stay seated.

"I'm just trying to help it go quicker!"

He shook his head. "You're worse than a small child!"

She shrugged. "I'm sorry." The truth was, no one had ever bothered to get to know her well enough to give her a gift that she cared about before. She knew Jack would be the first, and she couldn't wait to see what he'd done.

After her cake, she jumped up and put the dishes in the basin. "May I help you wash them?" she asked.

He sighed. "You can wipe. I'll wash."

She knew she could wash them faster, but she didn't protest. At least they'd finish faster by working together. "Leave the pot of stew for our supper."

He nodded, knowing better than to throw away that much food.

Finally, they finished. He turned to her. "Put your coat and mittens on."

She looked toward the bedroom door with a frown. "But..."

"Coat and mittens."

She decided not to argue, pulling her coat on quickly and buttoning it. She watched as he put his coat on as well. She had no idea where they were going, but she could tell he was going to be stubborn and insist they do whatever it was before they went into the bedroom for her surprise.

She pulled her mittens on and looked at him. "I'm ready."

He took her mittened hand in his. "Come on." He led her out to the small barn that was on the property. It was barely big enough to call a barn, but it housed one cow and two horses. He opened the big door leading into the building and waited for her to precede him.

As soon as the door opened, Coral could hear yelps. She squealed and hurried around Jack, rushing into the barn and stopping short as she saw a puppy pulling at a rope that was tied around his neck. "Oh, Jack! He's beautiful!"

She dropped to her knees and hugged the jumping, yelping dog to her. He was only about knee-high, but his feet were huge. He was going to be a big dog.

"Will that help you stay happy while I'm working?"

She jumped up and threw her arms around him, hugging him close. "I couldn't have asked for a better birthday gift. Thank you so much!"

Jack smiled, stroking her back. "I'm glad you like him. Do you want to take him inside with us when you see your other gift?"

"I can't believe there's more!"

He reached down and untied the puppy, leading him into the house. The animal was thrilled to be there, sniffing around everywhere exploring. After they'd both taken off their coats, he took her hand and led her to the bedroom door. "I'm not quite finished, but it's close enough for you to know what I'm doing. And really, I think you'll want to do the next part yourself."

She looked at him curiously, but didn't ask. Instead she waited as he opened the door and she peered inside. "Oh, Jack." Tears filled her eyes. No one had seen her cry since she'd been a small child, but she couldn't control herself. She stepped into the room and walked to the small book case he'd built for her, stroking it with her hand. "I can't wait to put my books on it."

He shook his head. "That's not your present."

She looked at him, the tears streaming freely down her face now. "It's not?"

"No, that's where you will *keep* your present." He indicated a large crate in the corner of the room.

She walked over to the crate and lifted the lid off. Her breath caught, and she sucked in a breath. "Jack! How—" She asked nothing else as she flew to him again, burying her face against the front of his shirt.

He held her to him, happy she'd reacted as he'd expected. "I love you with everything inside me, Coral Smythe."

She smiled up at him, pulling his head down for a kiss. "And I love you even more, Jackson Smythe! And I'm not just saying that because you got me a crate of medical books for my birthday!"

He grinned. "It's not all medical books."

"It's not?"

He shook his head. "No. It's mostly medical books, but there's one book on how to add a room to your home. I thought we could do that together this summer."

She smiled. "And what will we do with that room?"

"I think a new room is needed for a midwife's office, don't you? And we'll make sure there are bookshelves all around for your ever increasing library."

"Wait—you wouldn't mind if I opened a midwife practice?"

He shook his head. "It sounds like you've spent enough time learning under an experienced midwife. You know medical books better than most doctors. I made certain to get you books that would concentrate on pregnancy. Some are general knowledge, of course, but at least half are about the birthing process."

"Do you realize the gift you're giving me?" she asked softly. "Not just by giving me the books, but by telling me you don't mind if I work?"

He nodded. "I know what you want and need, because I *know* you. You are truly a marvel, Coral, and I'm not going to let you hide your accomplishments from the world. I don't want to share you, but you're too special. I don't have a choice."

The tears were flowing again, more freely than before, as she buried her face against his shirt. "I don't know what I've ever done to deserve you, Jack."

He held her to him. "It's I who am blessed to have you."

Epilogue

CORAL SAT ON THE EDGE of her sister's bed, wiping Esther's brow. "Trust you to do everything wrong, Esther. Do you just *try* to be difficult?"

Esther glared at her sister as she lay back, resting between pushes. "I'm not doing anything wrong! I'm having a baby!"

"Yes, but you're having an upside down baby. It's coming out feet first!"

Esther closed her eyes and laid back. "So now what?"

Coral shrugged. "I'm going to have to reach up and help him come out." She frowned. "I need you to wait until I tell you to push, and then I'll help guide him out. It's the only way."

"Just do it."

Coral didn't blame her sister for being grumpy. She'd been laboring for more than twenty-four hours, and they were both worn out.

Twenty minutes later, Coral handed the now-clean baby boy to his mother. "He's perfect, Esther. You did it."

Esther reached out and took Coral's hand in hers. "No. *We* did it. I'm so glad you were with me. Now you need to have a little boy, so my son can have a cousin."

Coral patted her round belly. She had two more months to go until her precious baby came into the world. "I don't know. I want a girl first."

"What does Jackson say?"

Coral grinned at that. "Jack? He says he wants a dozen little girls who will be just like their mother."

Esther smiled wearily. "I'm glad we came out here and found good men."

Coral smiled, knowing if their father had never been discovered to be embezzling money, and Esther's fiancé hadn't thrown her over, she would never have been able to be a midwife, and she certainly wouldn't have found happiness with a wonderful man like Jack. "I wouldn't change any of the events of the past thirteen months for the whole world." She stood. "I'm going to go get Brody. I think it's time he met his son."

For a full list of books by Kirsten Osbourne click here[1].

To sign up for Kirsten Osbourne's mailing list and receive notice of new titles as they are available, click here.[2]

---

1.   http://www.kirstenandmorganna.com/super-secret-link-page/

2.   http://eepurl.com/y6WRb